P9-DZM-257

Elmo Says,
"Don't Wake the Baby!"

By Constance Allen
Illustrated by David Prebenna

A GOLDEN BOOK • NEW YORK

Published by Golden Books Publishing Company, Inc.,
in conjunction with Children's Television Workshop

© 1997 Children's Television Workshop. Jim Henson's Sesame Street Muppet Characters © 1997 Jim Henson Productions, Inc. All rights reserved. Printed in the U.S.A. No part of this book may be reproduced or copied in any form without written permission from the copyright owner. Sesame Street and the Sesame Street Sign are trademarks and service marks of Children's Television Workshop. All other trademarks are the property of Golden Books Publishing Company, Inc., Racine, Wisconsin 53404. Library of Congress Catalog Card Number: 96-78714 ISBN: 0-307-10000-6 A MCMXCVII

"Oh, hello, Elmo!" said Natasha's mother one day. "I simply must get this penguin convention checked in. Would you be a dear and take Natasha for a walk around the block?"

"Sure!" said Elmo. "No trouble at all!"

"Just don't wake the baby, dear," said Natasha's mother.

TAP
TAP

Elmo and Natasha passed some construction workers.
The construction workers were making lots of noise.
"Hey!" shouted Elmo. "Please don't wake the baby!"

Natasha was still fast asleep.

Next they passed a traffic jam. Trucks honked and cars beeped.

"HEY!" shouted Elmo. "PLEASE DON'T WAKE THE BABY!"

BEEP
BEEP

BEEP

Natasha was still fast asleep.

A parade marched by. Music played, whistles blew, and feet stomped. It was very noisy.

"HEY!" shouted Elmo. "PLEASE DON'T WAKE THE BABY!"

Natasha was still fast asleep.

A jumble of bank robbers tumbled down the stairs of the
bank as an alarm bell clanged. It was very noisy.
"HEY!" shouted Elmo. "PLEASE DON'T WAKE THE BABY!"

Natasha was still fast asleep.

They passed a baseball game. CRACK! went a bat. ROAR!
went the crowd. It was very noisy.

"HEY!" shouted Elmo. "PLEASE DON'T WAKE THE BABY!"

HURRAY!

Natasha was still fast asleep. But then someone in the crowd hiccuped.

"*WAAHH*," said Natasha.

"Uh-oh," said Elmo. "HEY, EVERYONE!" he shouted. "PLEASE HELP ELMO MAKE THE BABY STOP CRYING!"

"Coo," said Natasha.

"KEEP IT UP, PLEASE, EVERYONE!" shouted Elmo. And, sure enough, Natasha stopped crying and fell back to sleep.

"Yoo-hoo, Elmo!" called Natasha's mother, as Elmo wheeled the carriage back to the Furry Arms. "Oh, look! The baby is still asleep. I hope she wasn't any trouble."

"No trouble at all," said the tired little monster.

"**ZZZZzz**," said Natasha.